Twilight
Fairies

June 2004

for the kids at
Hillcrest Elementary-
Wishing all of you
a little magic, each &
every day!

Nancy Hundal

With much love to my nieces and nephews:
Jordan, Carleigh, Taylor, Kellen, Amanda, Chelsea, Cassandra and Derrien.
May the magic of childhood remain with you always.
— N.H.

To Nancy, for traveling to the magical land of fairies with me.
— D.K.
Thanks to: Karisa, Charlie, Nicole, Lindsey

Text copyright © 2002 by Nancy Hundal
Illustrations copyright © 2002 by Don Kilby

Design by Wycliffe Smith Design

Published in Canada by Fitzhenry & Whiteside, 195 Allstate Parkway, Markham, Ontario L3R 4T8

Published in the United States by Fitzhenry & Whiteside, 121 Harvard Avenue, Suite 2, Allston, Massachusetts 02134

www.fitzhenry.ca   godwit@fitzhenry.ca.

10 9 8 7 6 5 4 3 2 1

National Library of Canada Cataloguing in Publication

Hundal, Nancy, 1957-
Twilight fairies / by Nancy Hundal ; illustrated by Don Kilby.

ISBN 1-55041-645-6 (bound).--ISBN 1-55041-786-X (pbk.)

I. Kilby, Don II. Title.

PS8565.U5635T85 2002   jC813'.54   C2002-901500-6
PZ7

U.S. Publisher Cataloging-in-Publication Data
(Library of Congress Standards)

Hundal, Nancy.
Twilight fairies / written by Nancy Hundal ; illustrated by Don Kilby.—1st ed.
[32] p. : col. ill. ;   cm.

Summary: Miranda's birthday celebration this year will be an evening garden party. And if she plans everything just right,
Miranda knows the fairies will join in. It doesn't matter that no one else believes that fairies will appear.
One girl's faith in their magic should be enough.

ISBN 1-55041-645-6
ISBN 1-55041-786-X (pbk.)

1. Fairies -- Fiction. 2. Magic – Fiction. 3. Birthdays – Fiction. I. Kilby, Don. II. Title.
[E] 21   2001   AC CIP

Fitzhenry & Whiteside acknowledges with thanks the Canada Council for the Arts, the Government of Canada
through the Book Publishing Industry Development Program (BPIDP), and the Ontario Arts Council
for their support for our publishing program.

Printed in Hong Kong.

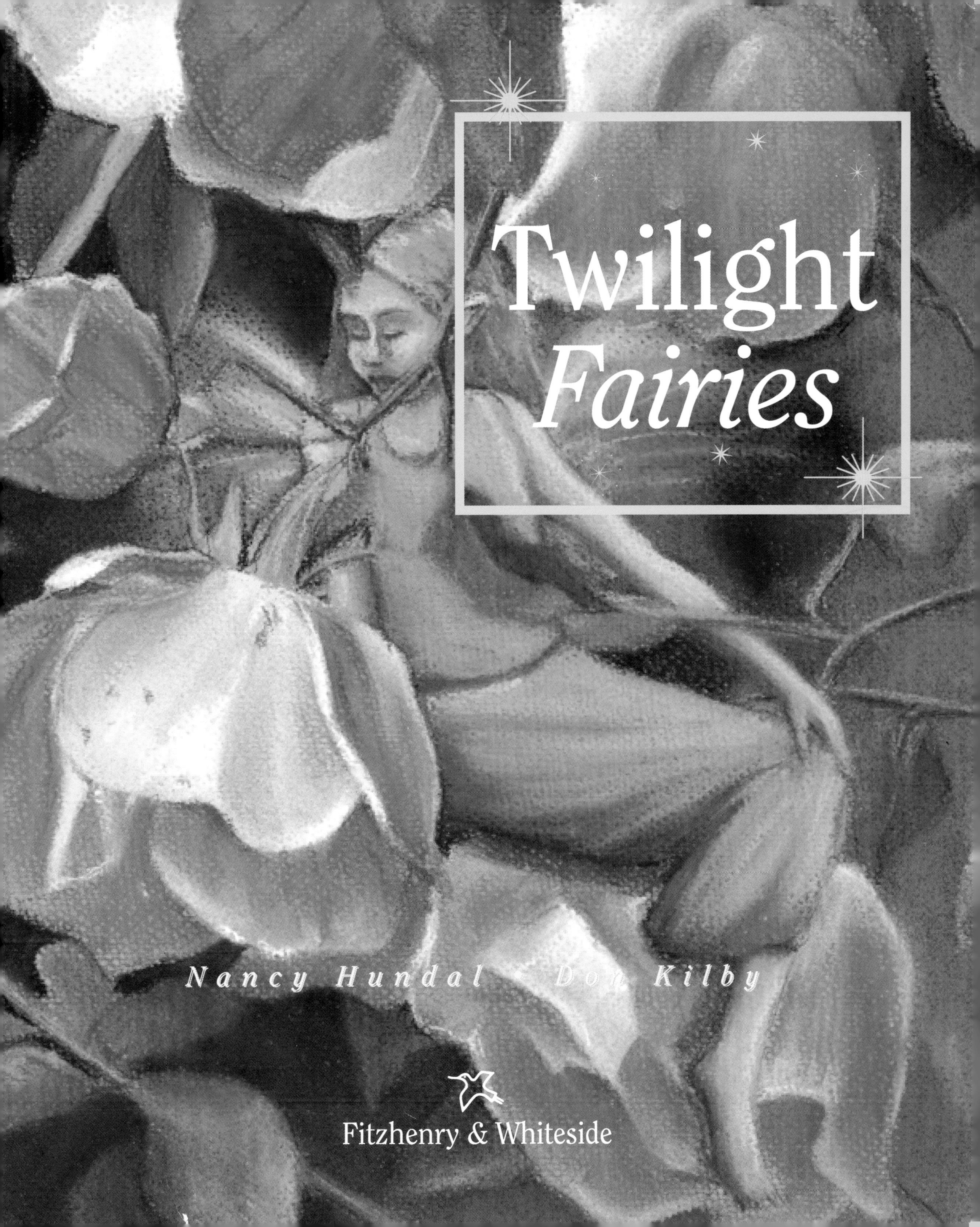

Twilight *Fairies*

Nancy Hundal • Don Kilby

Fitzhenry & Whiteside

nce upon a summer's memory,

there lived a girl called Miranda. She loved birthday

parties and garden fairies. And as it happened, the fairies

loved birthday parties too.

Miranda's garden was enchanting, enormous.
Her mother spent hours planting, pruning, pulling,
persuading. The plants heard, but did not answer.

Miranda delighted in helping, as here and there,
under fern or inside petal, she glimpsed fairy wings,
she heard fairy song.

She whispered and cooed at them. But like the
plants, they did not answer — for they were night
creatures and often slumbered the sunshine away.

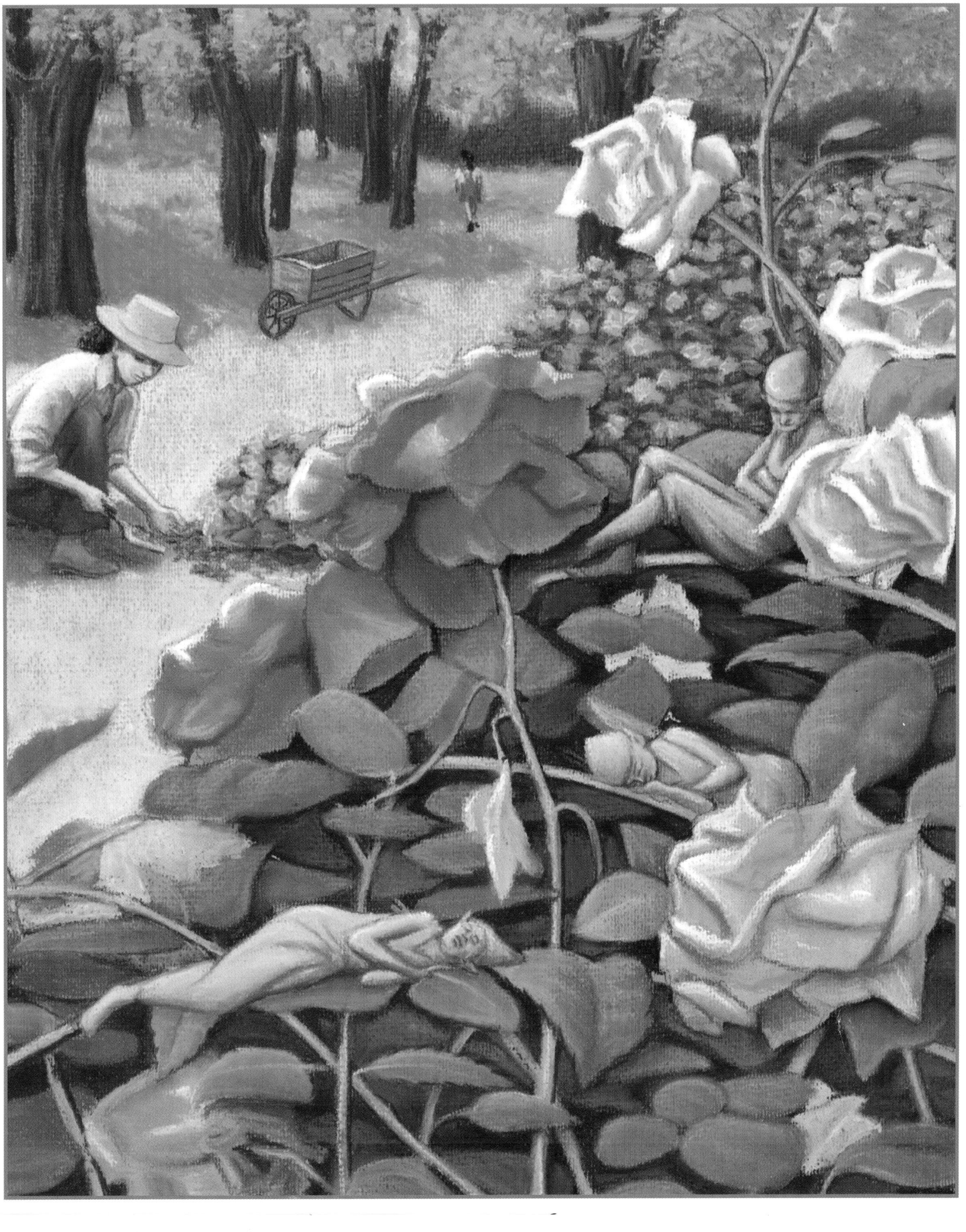

But with the twilight came the garden fairies,
creeping out to frolic in shadow, rub sleepydust
from crinkly eyes, and prepare for the mischief
and magic of deepest night.

They loved the raindrops, tickling…trickling over
their long, spiky hair, past pointy ears and chins…

…and the breezy summer nights, cobwebs swaying,
flowers waltzing, windstruck like the fairies.

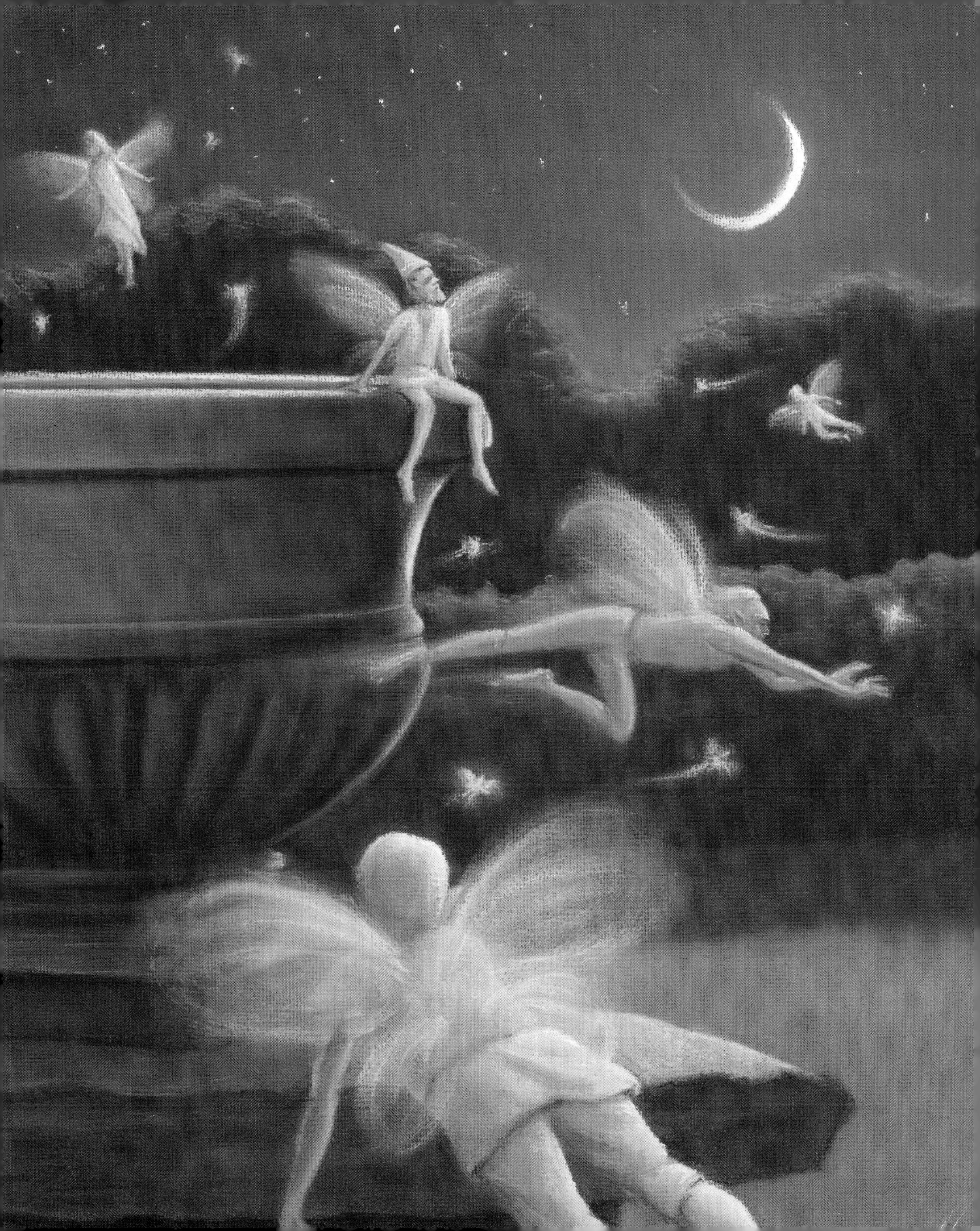

Miranda's birthday, at the very peak of summer, was near.

"Caitlin had a bowling party," older brother Sam remembered.

"And Courtney? Wasn't hers the magician?" added Mom. "What about yours, Miranda? Bowling? Swimming?"

"No, Mom," was Miranda's answer. "No bowling, no swimming. Just the garden, my friends and...the fairies."

Sam's lips folded themselves into a wobbly line, hiding the smile that almost wiggled out.

"Your fairies again?" Mom shot him a look that helped keep the smile hidden. "All right, Miranda. You shall have your garden party. But don't be disappointed if the fairies...stay away."

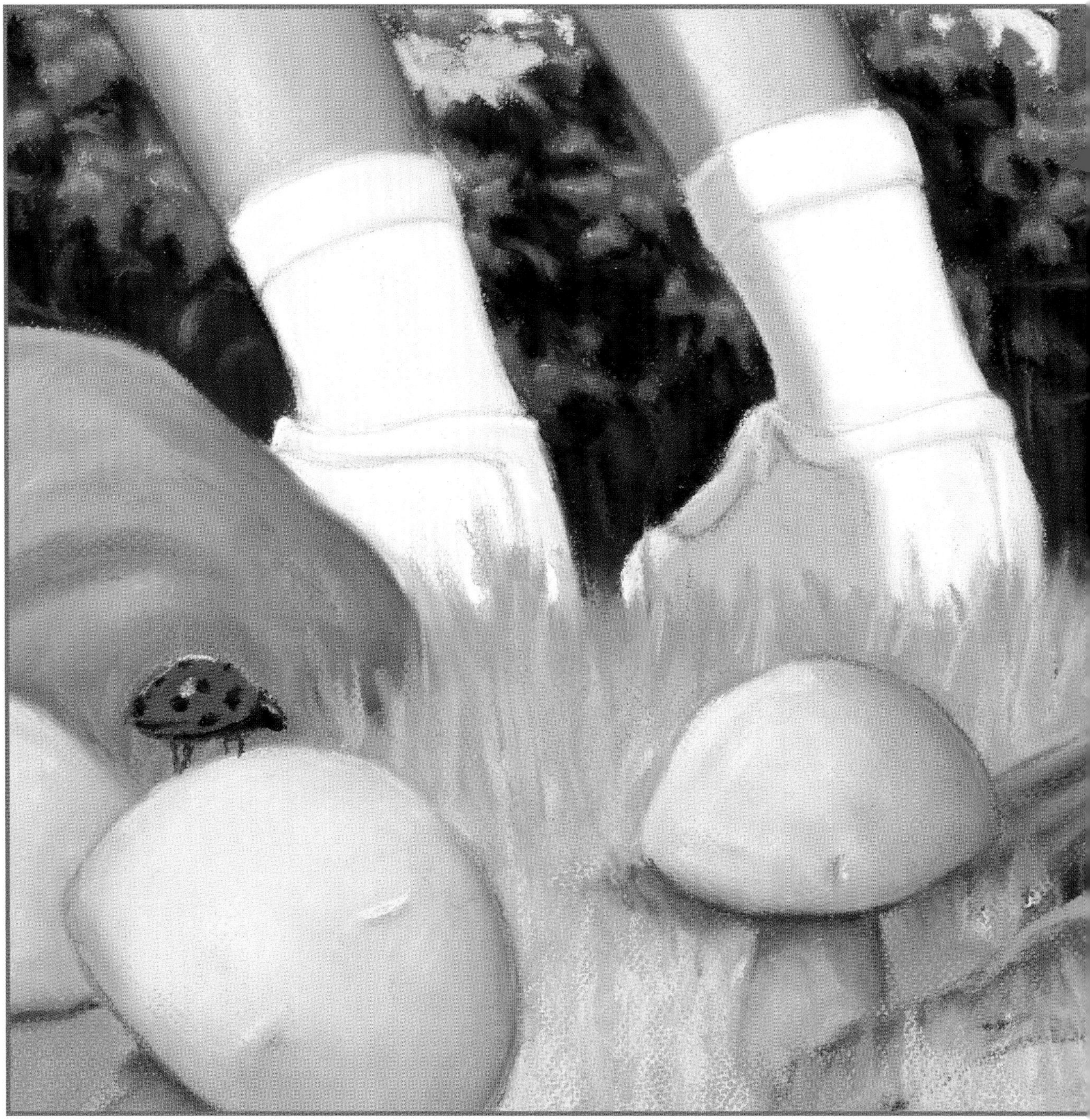

But Miranda knew better. The fairies lived, she'd learned, not in the front garden, where blooms rose on erect stems and leaves snapped together like soldiers at attention.

They gamboled farther back, where old cedar's fragrant shoulders drooped protectively around the garden below.

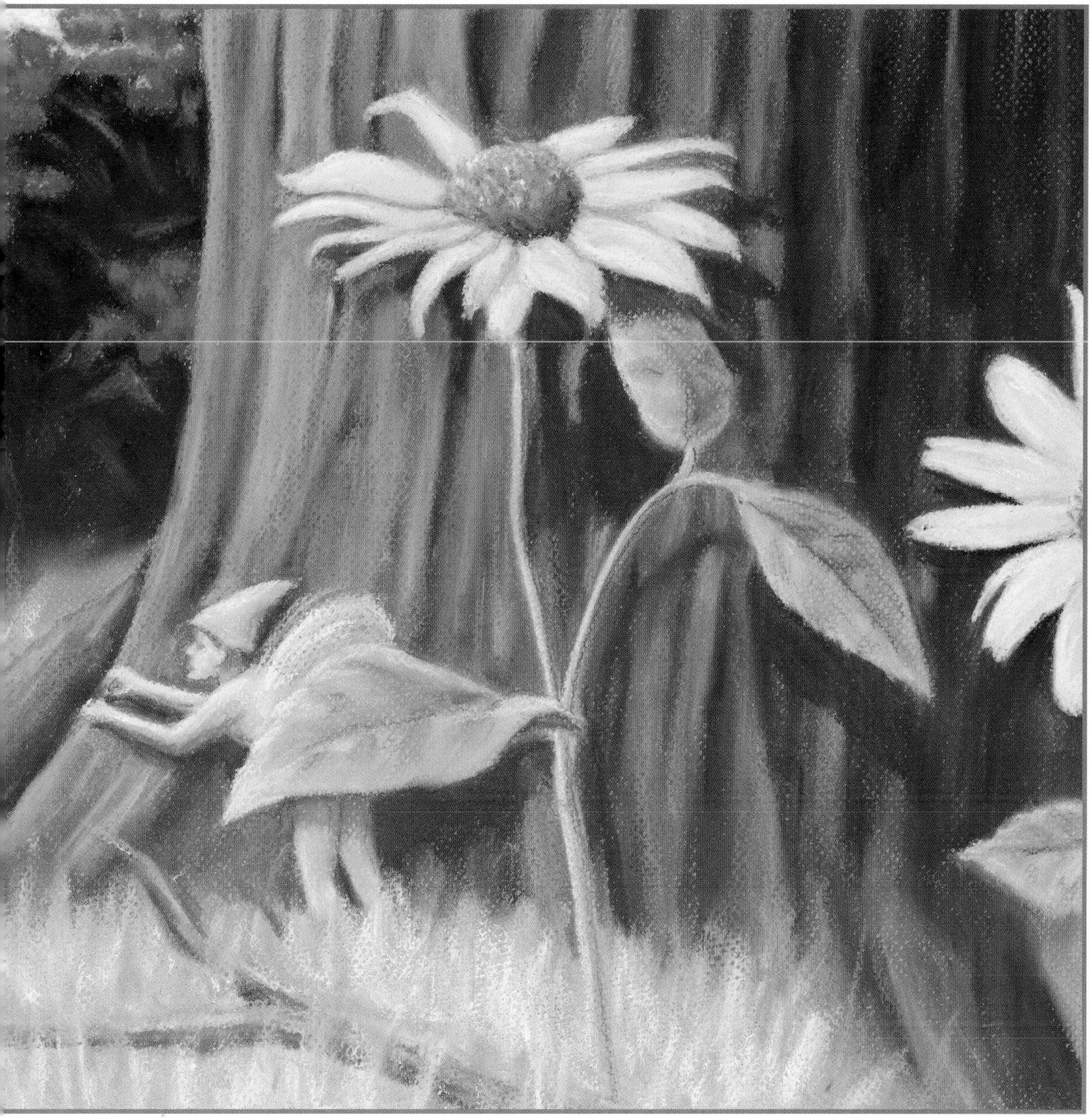

Back there, Miranda hid amongst the hodgepodge
of buttercups and daisies, thorny pink roses and pansies
of indigo velvet.

And there she planned her party, painted decorations,
printed invitations.

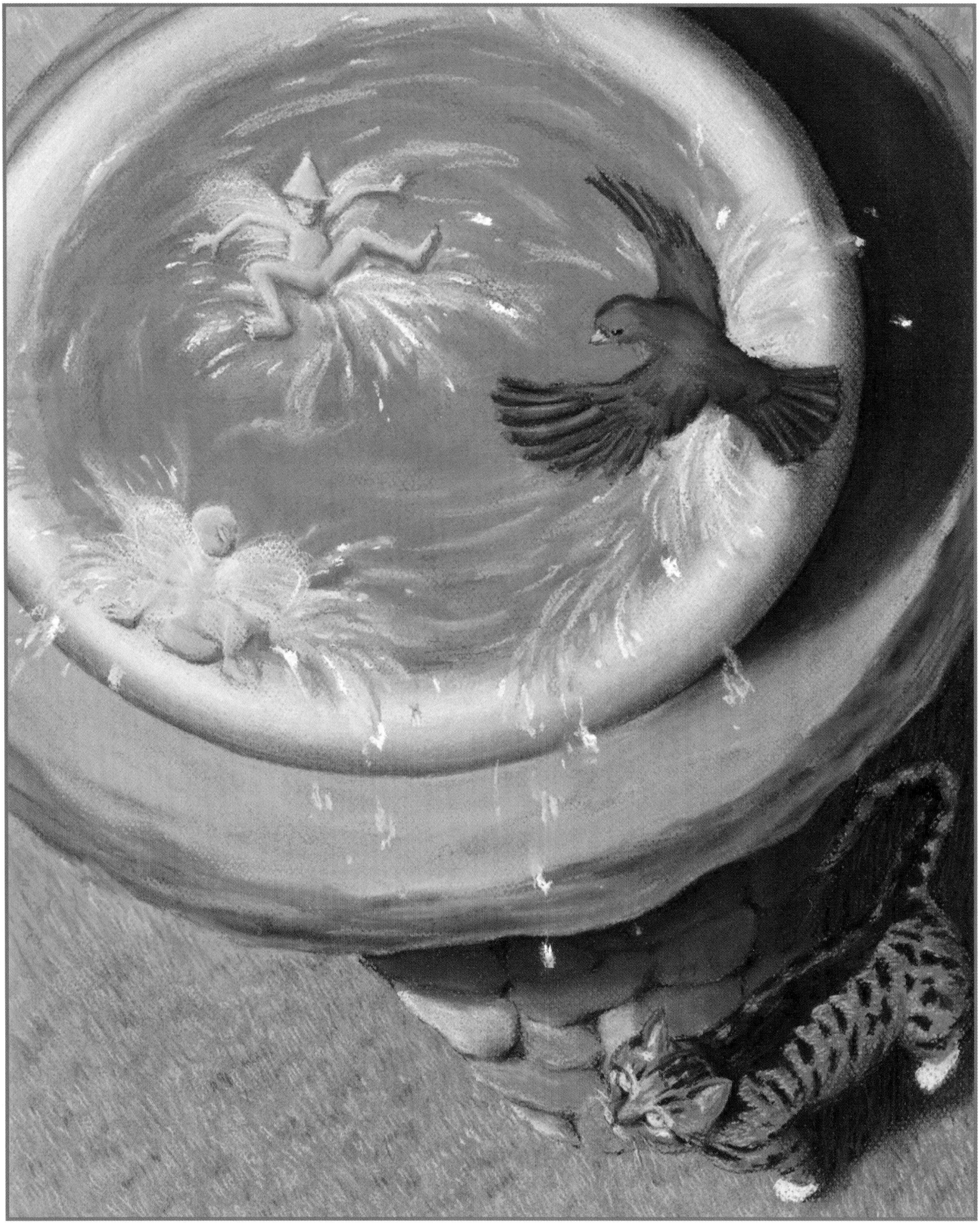

And she watched the cat meander amongst the blossoms, rubbing his archy back against the birdbath. He knew what was there—he gazed discreetly from yellow slitted eyes, but never caught even a silky wing.

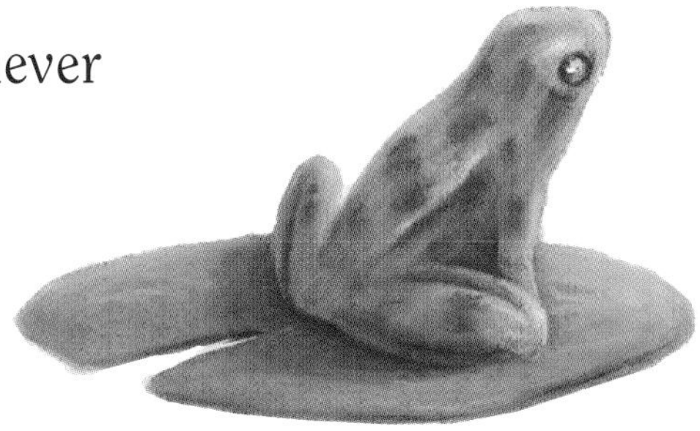

She watched the frogs,
leaping politely over fairy dust,
disturbing nothing. Miranda watched.

Mom made a cake, a circle of angel food frosted in pink, sugary bliss. She made dainty sandwiches of tomato and cucumber, pitchers of soursweet lemonade. Hot dogs and fairies do not mix.

It was Miranda's turn to toil in the garden. She puffed air into pastel balloons, suspended them from tree branches. Giant pearly dewdrops, quivering, waiting.

Even Sam helped, climbing the ladder to string loops of green crepe paper between the trees.

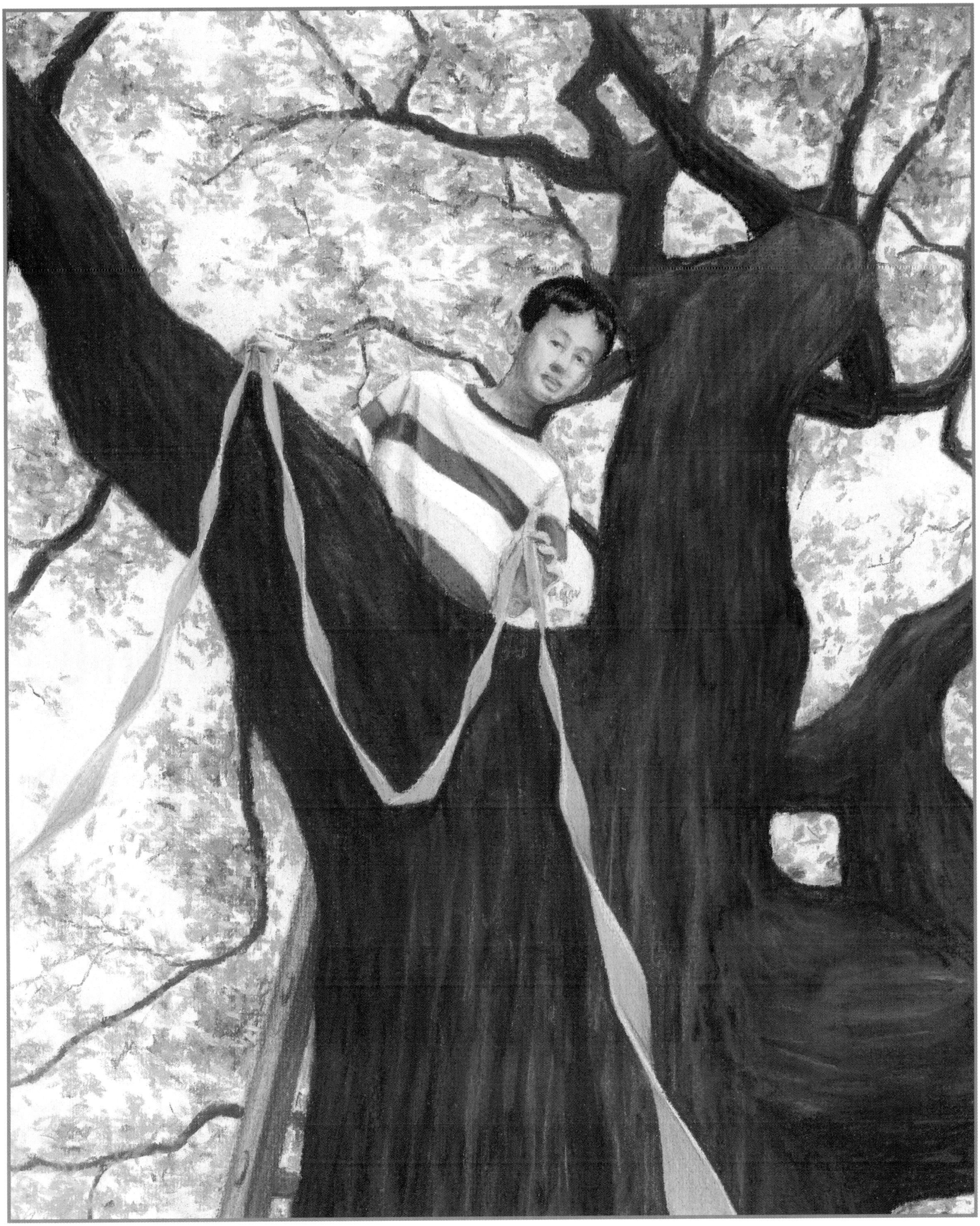

When Sam was gone, Miranda spoke. "Do you think my friends will like my party?" she wondered aloud, hoping to catch a fairy's ear. "Will it seem old-fashioned and silly?" And then, in a quieter voice, "Please come too. All of you."

She didn't think to plan games, for she knew that Pin-The-Tail-On-The-Anything would be out of place at her enchanted birthday.

And so at midsummer,
as afternoon passed into twilight,
Miranda's friends arrived. It was
their very first evening birthday.

Miranda's dress, of palest green satin,
shimmered as the twinkly lights
in the garden's trees came on.

Caitlin and Courtney's eyes lit too, when they saw

the back garden. Now, gossamer threads hung between

the trees; the balloons were dusted with whorls of sparkle;

and wildflowers, arranged in tiny vases, were everywhere.

Mom gasped. Sam gasped. Even Miranda gasped,

though she knew that fairy dust was a strange and

powerful tool.

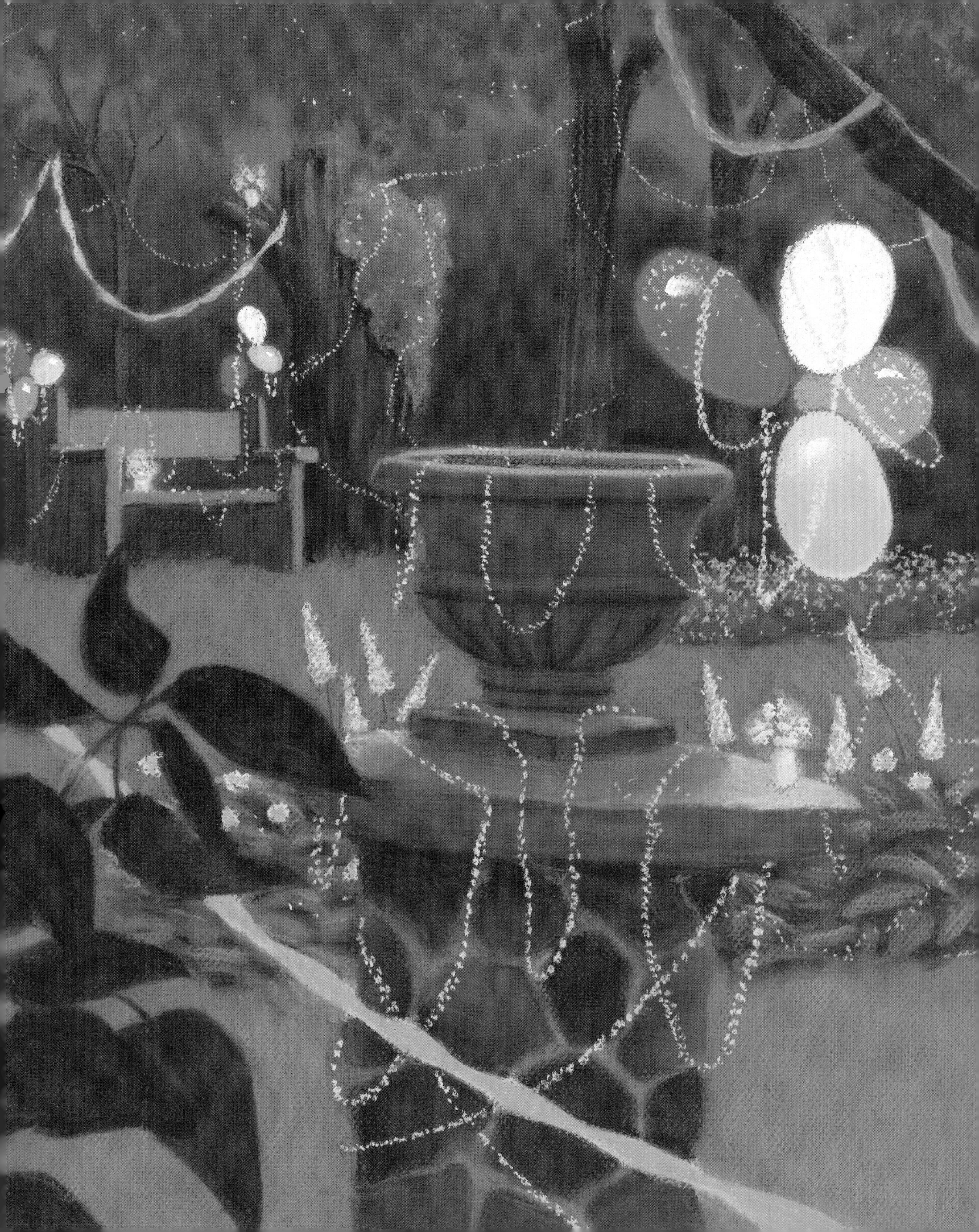

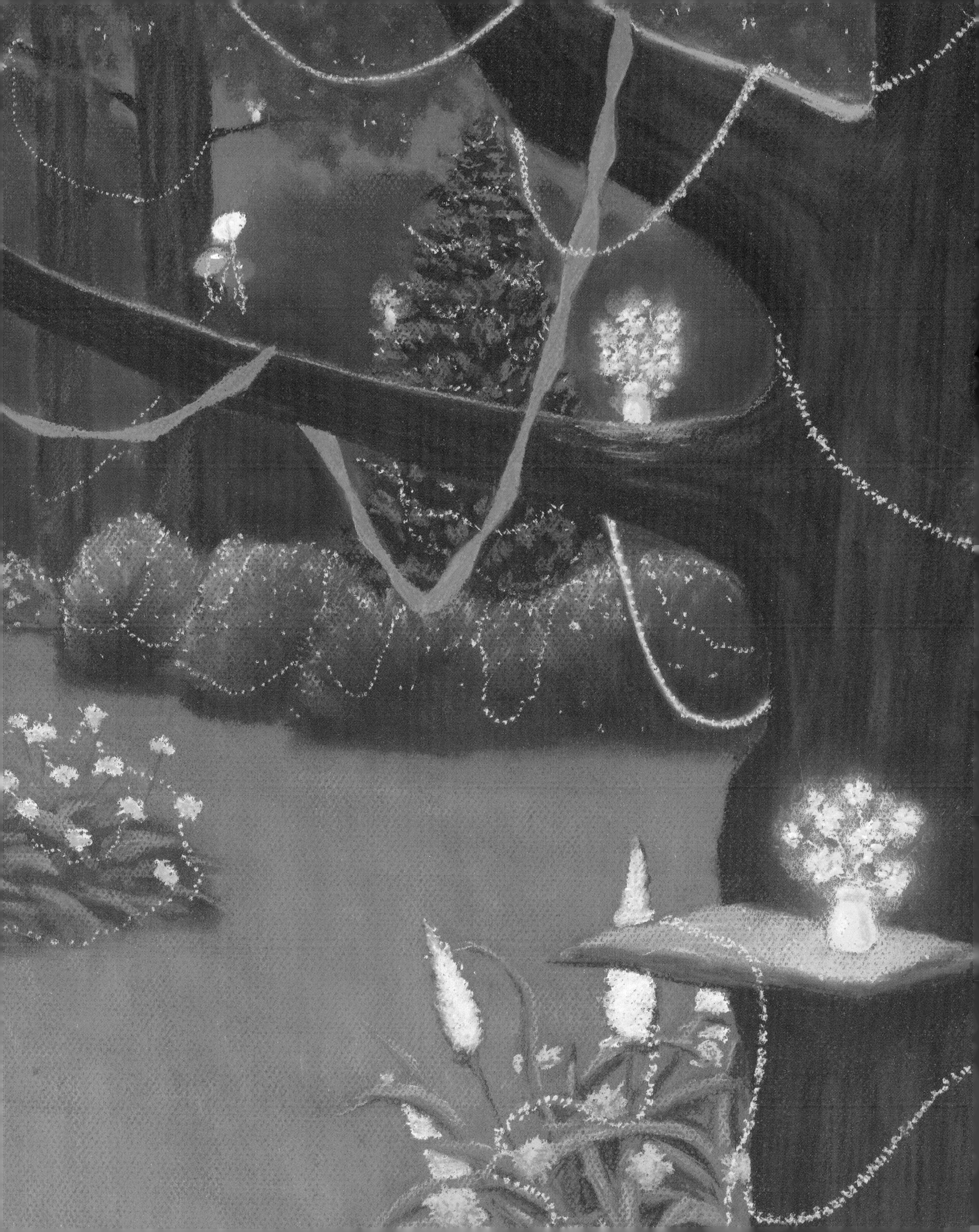

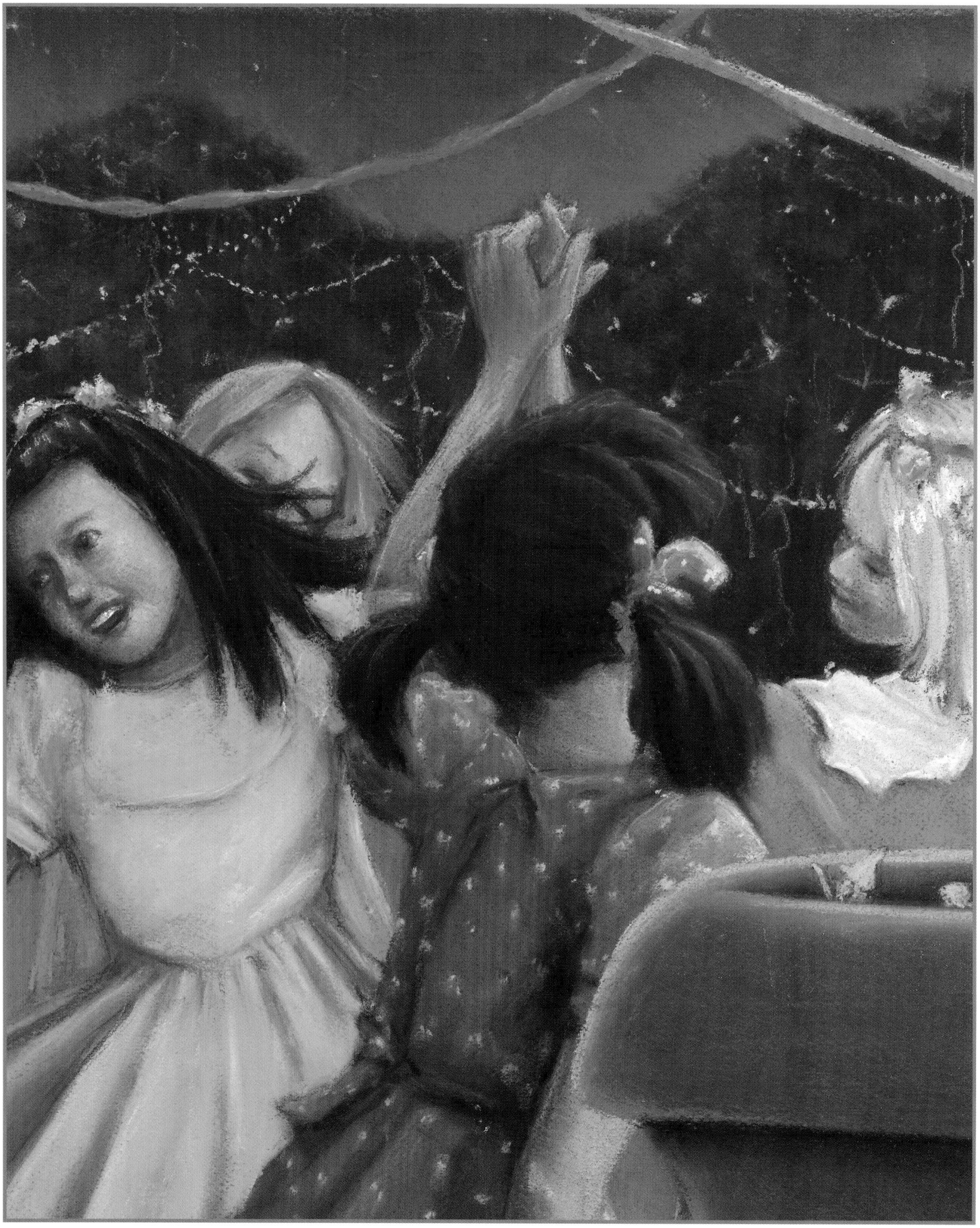

It was a glorious evening. The girls played hide-and-seek in the shadows, and sang high, sweet melodies together, their voices wafting up to the stars.

They licked frosting from their fingers, and felt the perfumed breezes of night rustle against their cheeks. Not once did they think of bowling balls or card tricks, not even once.

Miranda could hear the tinklehum of fairymerrymaking as she passed her cake, opened her gifts. But she kept the fairy guests her own special secret. Those born at midsummer can keep such secrets well.

Later, as moonbeams slanted through the cedar tree, her friends departed. Miranda waved each a sleepy farewell. Fairy dust weighed down her eyelids, but buoyed up her heart.

"Good night, Miranda," said Mom. She left Miranda with a soft kiss and an even softer glance, remembering now her own enchanted girlhood.

Sam scratched his head, then patted Miranda's. His glance was curious, wondering.

"Good night, Sam," Miranda said, eyes glowing.

Long after the last goodbye, the fairies darted amongst the birthday clutter, nibbling at crumbs of sugary frosting, tying bits of discarded ribbon into their hair.

At her window, Miranda glimpsed sparkles floating in the back garden and knew that, although her party was over, the fairies' was not.

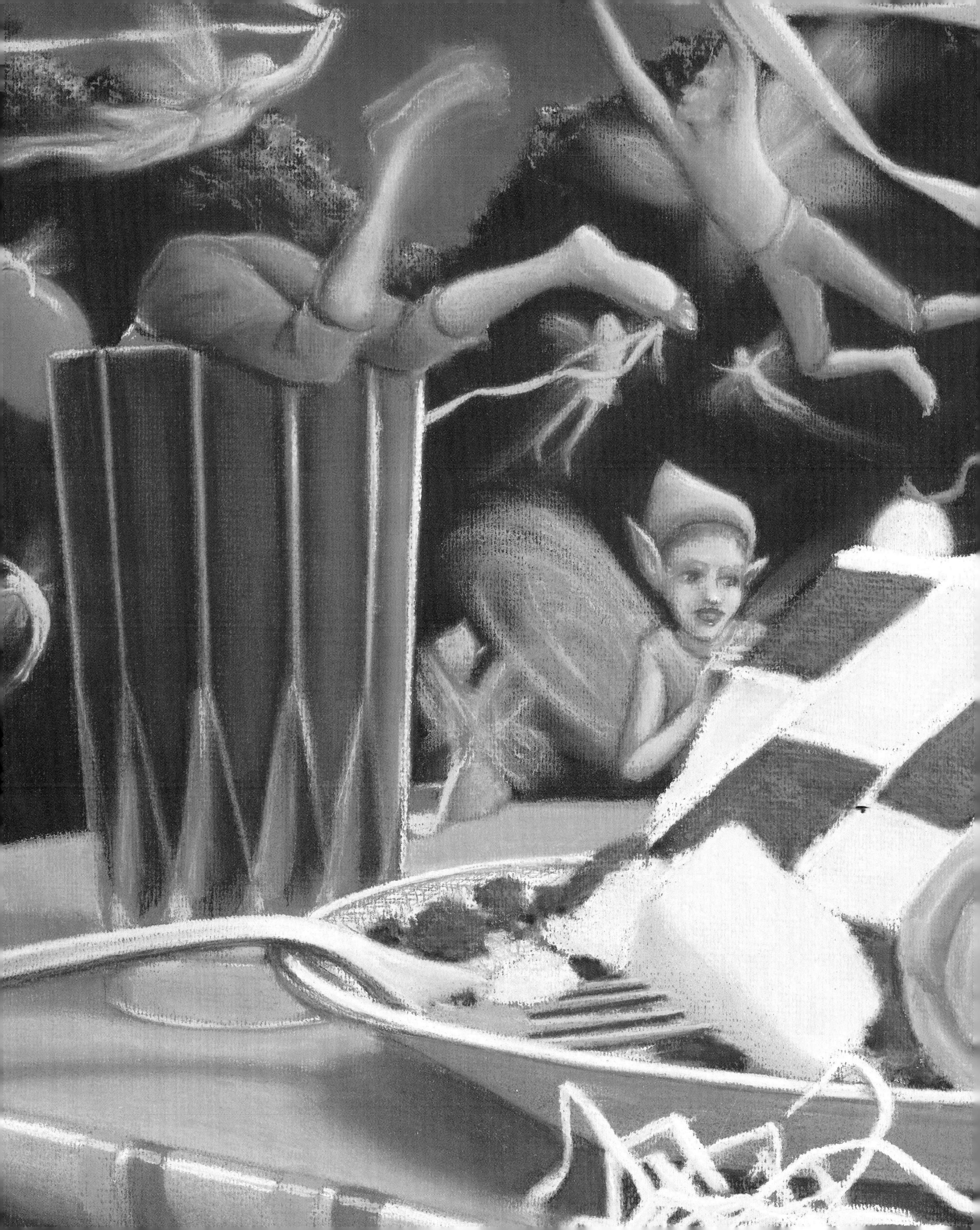

A fairy tune, sung high and shimmery, finally lulled her to sleep. The fairies hovered at the window until her dreams led her off.

Midsummer was past. The twilight party was over.

Though Miranda is now an old, old woman,
she loves garden parties to this day.

And she and the fairies frolic on her birthday
every midsummer's eve. Still.